This book belongs to:

....

....

To my twoo love, Hannah.
- I.C.

BROWN OWL BOOKS

First published in Great Britain in 2022 by Brown Owl Books.

© 2022 Ian Curran

A CIP catalogue record for this book is available from the British Library.

HB ISBN: 978 1 915678 00 3
PB ISBN: 978 1 915678 01 0
E-Book ISBN: 978 1 915678 02 7

Printed and bound in China

www.iancurran.com

THE OWL THAT COULD ONLY TWIT

Ian Curran

Illustrated by James Cottell

A little, brown owl sat alone in the dark,
In the middle of a tree, in the middle of a park.
She could hear on the breeze, as a soft wind blew
The calling of the owls, **"twit twoo, twit twoo."**
But Little Brown Owl thought her heart might break,
As that was a sound she just could not make.
She tried and she tried every night and day,
But **'twoo'** was a word she just could not say.

She could **'twit'** alright. She could **'twit'** all night long.
But without the **'twoo'** she felt rightfully wrong.
Little Brown Owl decided there and then
That she never, ever wanted to feel that way again.

She thought and she thought about what she could do,
And if there might be a place where owls find their own **'twoo'**.
So, she spread out her wings and lifted her head,
And Little Brown Owl took a deep breath and said . . .

"I must be brave, and I must be strong.
I must believe there's a place I belong.
I don't know how far, and I don't know the way,
So I'll aim for the stars. Up! Up! And away!"

Little Brown Owl set off through the dark,
From the middle of her tree, in the middle of her park.
She flew and she flapped, and she flapped and she flew,
On an adventure to find her own **'twoo'**.

She flew high over hospitals, houses and hills,
And looked down on museums and meadows and mills.
She flew for so long her wings started to ache.
Then she spotted a spot she could stop for a break.

She swooped down and landed on a green, garden shed
And startled a hedgehog who was making his bed.

"Oh, hello Little Brown Owl. Such a beautiful night.
But you do look sad. Are you quite alright?"

Little Brown Owl looked down from the roof
And started to tell Mr Hedgehog the truth.
"Wherever I go I don't seem to fit.
I'm so sad and lonely," said the owl that could only twit.

Mr Hedgehog listened, which was awfully nice,
Then gave Little Brown Owl some friendly advice.
"Don't worry yourself over one little '**twoo**',
Think of the bigger things little you can do."

"Like what?" said the owl, who was getting upset.
Mr Hedgehog replied, "Well now, don't you forget
You have smooth, silky feathers. You're softer than rugs.
You could make lots of friends and have lots of hugs."

Little Brown Owl thought about that a while,
And for the first time in a long time, she started to smile.
"Thank you, Mr Hedgehog. You've been ever so kind.
But I still think it's something that I need to find."

So, she spread out her wings and lifted her head,
And Little Brown Owl took a deep breath and said . . .

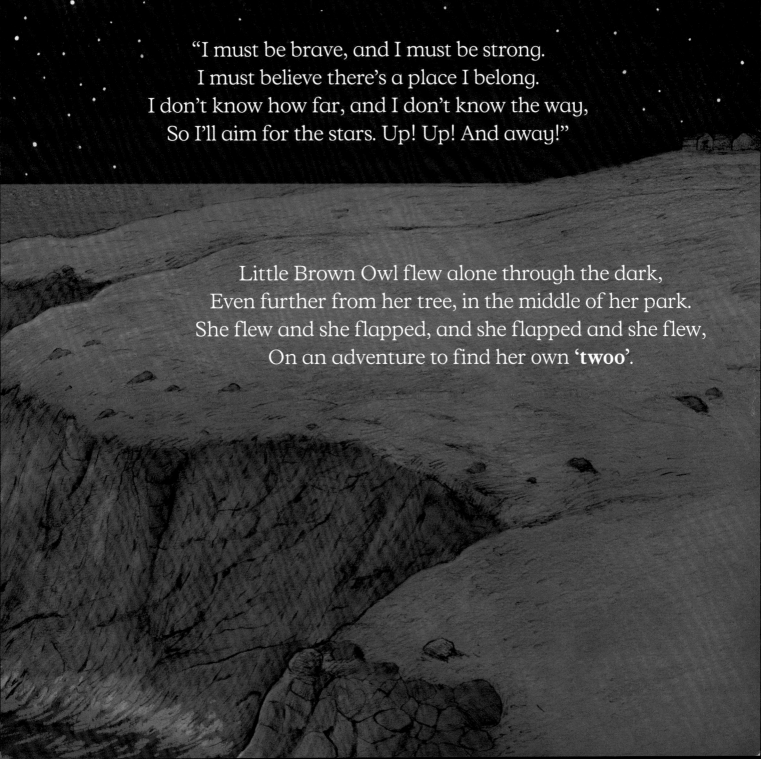

"I must be brave, and I must be strong.
I must believe there's a place I belong.
I don't know how far, and I don't know the way,
So I'll aim for the stars. Up! Up! And away!"

Little Brown Owl flew alone through the dark,
Even further from her tree, in the middle of her park.
She flew and she flapped, and she flapped and she flew,
On an adventure to find her own **'twoo'**.

She flew high over lighthouses, lampposts and lanes,
And looked down on tall towers and town halls and trains.
She flew for so long, her wings started to ache.
Then she spotted a spot she could stop for a break.

She swooped down and landed on a short, wooden post,
Unsettling a badger who was eating some toast.

"Oh, hello Little Brown Owl. Such a beautiful night.
But you do look sad. Are you quite alright?"

Little Brown Owl looked down from the stumps
And explained why she seemed to be down in the dumps.
"I've tried and I've tried, and I still cannot see
How every owl can do it, except for little me."

Mrs Badger listened, which was awfully nice,
Then gave Little Brown Owl some familiar advice.
"Don't worry yourself over one little '**twoo**'.
Think of the bigger things little you can do."

"Like what?" said the owl, with a tear in her eye.
Mrs Badger replied, "You can fly! You can fly!

You can travel the world with your wonderful wings.
You can go to lots of places and see lots of things."
Little Brown Owl thought about that a while,
And for the second time that night, she started to smile.

"Thank you, Mrs Badger. You've been ever so kind.
But I still think it's something that I need to find."
So, she spread out her wings and lifted her head,
And Little Brown Owl took a deep breath and said . . .

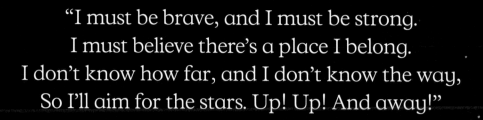

"I must be brave, and I must be strong.
I must believe there's a place I belong.
I don't know how far, and I don't know the way,
So I'll aim for the stars. Up! Up! And away!"

Little Brown Owl flew alone through the dark,
So very far from her tree, in the middle of her park.
She flew and she flapped, and she flapped and she flew,
On an adventure to find her own **'twoo'**.

She flew high over skyscrapers, stables and schools,
And looked down on palaces and playgrounds and pools.
She flew for so long her wings started to ache.
Then she spotted a spot she could stop for a break.

She swooped down and landed on a telephone box,
And frightened a foraging, furry-tailed fox.

"Oh, hello Little Brown Owl. Such a beautiful night.
But you do look sad. Are you quite alright?"
Little Brown Owl looked down from the phone
And spoke about how it felt being alone.

"All the other owls leave me on the shelf,
So I end up **'twit, twitting'** all by myself."
Mr Fox listened, which was awfully nice,
Then gave Little Brown Owl some famous advice.

"Don't worry yourself over one little **'twoo'**.
Think of the bigger things little you can do."
"Like what?" said the owl, who was losing all faith.
Mr Fox replied, "Well, you'll always be safe.

Your ears can hear the quietest sound,
And your head can turn almost all the way round."
Little Brown Owl thought about that a while,
But this time she couldn't quite manage a smile.

"Thank you, Mr Fox. You've been ever so kind.
Perhaps it is something I'm not meant to find."
So, she spread out her wings and lifted her head,
And Little Brown Owl took a deep breath and said . . .

"I don't feel brave, and I don't feel strong.
I don't believe there's a place I belong.
I've travelled all night; it will soon become day.
I need to find somewhere safe I can stay."

She flew and she flapped, and she flapped and she flew,
And gave up all hope of finding her **'twoo'**.

She swooped into a nook through a hole in the bark,
In the middle of a tree, in the middle of a park.
She nestled inside and got ready for bed.
Then Little Brown Owl took a deep sigh and said . . .

"I don't want to be different. I just want to fit.
But who could ever love an owl that could only say **'twit'**?"
"Twoo!" came a sound from across the park.
"Twoo! Twoo!" seemed to echo through the trees in the dark.

Little Brown Owl was a little surprised
When she peered from the nook and opened her eyes.
As there, through the mist, came the wonderful sight . . .

Of a little, grey owl approaching mid-flight.
He flew and he flapped, and he flapped and he flew,
And replied to each **'twit'** with a very loud **'TWOO'**.

He swooped in and landed on a branch overhead.
Then the little, grey owl took a deep breath and said . . .

"Hello Little Brown Owl. I've been searching for you.
You see, I'm the owl that can only say '**twoo**'."

Little Brown Owl thought about that a while,
And from that very moment hasn't once lost her smile.
They stayed side-by-side, two birds of a feather,
And wherever they went, they went there together.

They built a beautiful nest that was cosy and dark,
In the middle of their tree, in the middle of their park.
Whenever she would **'twit'**, he'd be there with a **'twoo'**,
And they did all of the bigger things the two of them could do.

They travelled the world and made lots of friends.
They've had lots of hugs and when this story ends . . .
If you ever hear a **'twit-twoo'** from above,
It might be Little Brown Owl and her one **'twoo'** love.

Ian Curran

Ian grew up in Manchester, England, and has always loved writing stories. He graduated with a BA Hons in English Literature from The University of Sheffield and is now a member of The Society of Children's Book Writers and Illustrators (SCBWI).

Ian loves the theatre and has also written plays and musicals for the stage. Ian has lived in lots of different countries and travelled the world performing as an actor and presenter. He now lives back in Manchester with his wife, Hannah and his son, James.

To find out more or to book Ian for a school visit, please go to www.iancurran.com.